Short Horror Stories
Supernatural Stories That Are Scarier Than the Dead

Mildred T. Walker

Table of Contents
Bluesource And Friends 3

Description 4

Introduction 7

One: The Fall of the House of Usher 9

Two: The Monkey's Paw 23

Three: Ligeia 35

Four: The Lake 43

Five: The Legend of Sleepy Hollow 50

Conclusion 74

Bluesource And Friends

This book is brought to you by Bluesource And Friends, a happy book publishing company.

Our motto is **"Happiness Within Pages."**

We promise to deliver amazing value to readers with our books.

We also appreciate honest book reviews from our readers.

Connect with us on our Facebook page www.facebook.com/bluesourceandfriends and stay tuned to our latest book promotions and free giveaways.

Don't forget to claim your FREE book

https://tinyurl.com/karenbrainteasers

Also check out our best seller book

https://tinyurl.com/lateralthinkingpuzzles

Description

Are you looking for some old school scary stories? Do the newer scary stories being published today just not do the trick for you? If you answered yes to either of these questions, then *Short Horror Stories: Supernatural Stories That Are Scarier Than the Dead* is the right book for you.

Within this book, you will find some of the works of some of the greatest horror fiction writers that history has to offer, including Edgar Allan Poe's The Fall of the House of Usher, W.W. Jacob's The Monkey's Paw, Poe's Ligeia, Ray Bradbury's The Lake, and finally, Washington Irving's The Legend of Sleepy Hollow. These works may be old, but they have a staying power that transcends any of the literary trends of our age or any others.

Horror fiction is, and likely will always be, one of the most popular forms of fiction in the world. This genre has its roots in the early Greco-Roman people and has stood the test of time for thousands of years now, hardly ever wavering throughout all of history's many vicissitudes.

Fear is the most powerful emotion that we face as humans. Of all of the things that we get afraid of, there is one thing that affects us most profoundly across all of these areas: the fear of the unknown. In reading horror fiction, we are putting ourselves up against all of the things that we are unaware of, which may not only put us in a state of unease in the short term but also makes us analyze what is going on around us more closely and leads to long-term enlightenment.

The plots and characters throughout this collection of short stories vary widely, from haunted houses and cursed knick knacks, to dead brides coming back to life and headless horsemen. These are, again, some of the best horror authors that history has to offer, so be ready for anything when reading their works.

While these works may be the older ones, these authors are some of the most famous and successful in American literary history. All too often, scary story collections are filled with the works of dilettantes, but here we have stuck only to the classics. Let's hope you find these stories enjoyable. Thank you again for downloading *Short Horror Stories: Supernatural Stories That Are Scarier Than the Dead.*

Introduction

Congratulations and thank you for downloading *Short Horror Stories: Supernatural Stories That Are Scarier Than the Dead*. Within this book, we are going to go through some of the most terrifying stories ever written, all composed by the original American masters of horror fiction—Ray Bradbury, Washington Irving, W.W. Jacobs, and, of course, the great Edgar Allen Poe.

Horror fiction is one of the most popular and well-loved forms of fiction in the world. Its roots lie in antiquity with the Greeks and the Romans and perhaps even further back. Usually, this genre is known for its tendency to shock and surprise its audience, but it also maintains the ability to make people feel disgusted, repulsion, and or loathing, depending on what the author has in mind. It is the ability to draw on these more deeply negative emotions that sets horror as a genre apart from others in fiction. While we never want to initiate these feelings for ourselves, there is always some compelling force in reading works that makes us feel these ways that keep us invested, despite how badly we may want to look away at times.

These authors are, of course, some of the greatest horror authors in history, so we are being given a special treat in these works in particular. Here, we will read Edgar Allan Poe's The Fall of the House of Usher, W.W. Jacob's The Monkey's Paw, Poe's Ligeia, Ray Bradbury's The Lake, and finally, Washington Irving's The Legend of Sleepy Hollow.

Do not read any of these stories just before going to bed. While these are all older plots, they still have lots of resonance in just how scary they really are.

One: The Fall of the House of Usher

By: Edgar Allan Poe

It was a dark and soundless day in the depths of autumn. I was passing through the dreary countryside on horseback when I finally came across The House of Usher. An insufferable gloom passed over me as I saw the house with its bleak walls, eye-like windows, and its utter depression of the soil around it. I could not pinpoint just what it was about the house that made me feel this way. Sometimes, it is a vast combination of factors within a natural landscape or scene that coalesces to make a body feel uneasy, and it makes it so hard to find exactly what is causing the emotion.

Regardless of how this house made me feel, I had already made my mind to stay there for a few weeks. Its owner, Roderick Usher, had been one of my better companions in boyhood, but since then, I had not seen him at all. I had recently received a letter from Mr. Usher. In this letter, he informed me of a mental disorder that he had developed. He went on to say that my company would be very much welcomed because he had no one else to be around and because this would help him cope with his malady. I could not hesitate when I received this letter; I went immediately to his house.

Usher had always been a fairly-reserved person and came from a long line of great artists whose reputations for charity and devotion to detail had long been established in the area. The entire Usher family had no established branches in it, and therefore had a direct line of descent. This meant that the House eventually became synonymous with the family among the peasantry that worked on the property, because only the sons would inherit it generation after generation, with little to no variance in this trend.

The more I looked at this dreary house, the more it frightened me. It felt as if everything that I was seeing was only worsening the overall expression of the dismal place. The more time that I spent in front of the property looking out at the air around it, the more I started to get the impression that the whole property had a completely different atmosphere surrounding it than that of all of the circumjacent houses. While all of the other properties around the area seemed to be imbued with the atmosphere of the heavens, this one seemed to be imbued with that of the decayed trees surrounding it. The pestilent and mystic vapor that surrounded the place commiserate my feelings here.

I thought that I must have been dreaming, so I started to investigate the appearance further and saw that the house was very old and covered in fungi and spider webs on its interior. There was a generalized decay that prevailed the house, and the moving of the fabric within its window sills gave a sense of instability.

I then rode over a short causeway to the house. A servant met me at the front door. He led me to the master's studio, through rooms with somber tapestries on the walls, ebon blackness on the floors, and armorial trophies all over. All of these things I had been accustomed to seeing since childhood, by within this context, they gave off a different air about themselves. On one of the staircases that I passed by, I met the family's physician. He accosted me briefly and then passed on his way. The servant and I were now at the entrance of the master's study.

The room we entered was large, with encrimsoned light pouring in through dark draperies along all of the walls and windows. The furniture was old and uncomfortable, and everything about the room had a stern and gloomy air about it.

Upon entering the room, Roderick Usher greeted me with warmth. We sat down, and I could hardly recognize him. I doubt that I have ever seen a man who had changed so much throughout life since childhood as this one had. He had a cavernous face with large, liquid eyes and very thin and pallid lips. Altogether, it was a countenance that could have never been forgotten.

Usher's actions oscillated between extremely vivacious ones and extremely sullen ones. This oscillation was caused by his repeated efforts to overcome his habitual timidity. His voice did the same, with lots of statements coming out abruptly and with no effort and others biding their time and others being self-balanced, cool, and all together collected. Any outsider who was not already familiar with him would have likely mistaken him for an opium eater throughout his periods of excitement or a drunk throughout his periods of gloom.

He began by telling me that he had wanted to see me and about the solace I would provide for him. He then went on to describe his mental illness, which ran in his family for generations. He always ran on the anxiety/depression end of the spectrum, and this had only gotten worse in proportion to the square of the time he had spent alone. He also mentioned that the acuity of his senses was increasing as he got older, and went on to complain about this happening.

There was yet another aspect of his mental illness that I was just starting to notice. He seemed to have an unusual amount of superstitions surrounding the house he lived in. He had felt for years that there were things beyond his power of explanation going on in the house, which were being brought upon the morale of his existence, making his mental state deteriorate even more so.

There was one more problem that he went on about. This one he claimed had more of an effect on his overall well-being than any of the happenings of the house. This problem was the severe and long-continued illness of his beloved sister. She had been his sole companion for years, so her affliction was almost as detrimental to him as his own. She was the only relative that he had, so her decease would make him the last living Usher in the world. As we spoke of her, I saw her passing through one of the rooms, though she did not see me. Her sight filled me simultaneously with both a sense of astonishment and one of dread.

The sister went by the name of lady Madeline, and her disease baffled every physician she had come into contact with. In general, her disposition was marked by a settled apathy, a gradual wasting away of a person, and mild catalepsy, all of which made her at once severely disabled and altogether disagreeable to be around.

Throughout the next several days, nothing was said of lady Madeline among Mr. Usher and myself, and I busied myself primarily instead with making Usher feel better, as he was in a rather melancholic mood throughout this time. We spent this time mostly reading and painting, and the more I got to know the current Mr. Usher, the more I detested the idea of trying to lift his spirits up because darkness simply pervaded every thought and every perception of his, even those pertaining to the greatest things. While I will always remember this solemn time I spend with Mr. Usher, I will never be able to recall what exactly I was studying throughout the course of these days.

There was one thing that stuck out about this house in particular, and that was a long tunnel that had been covered up by a small picture at its entrance. Within this tunnel, there were no discernable light sources, but rays from the outside would illuminate its entire depth when uncovered.

It was at this point that Mr. Usher started to extol an opinion that he and others subscribed to. This opinion in itself did not surprise me, but the pertinacity with which he held this believe left me nonplussed. This opinion was that all vegetable things had sentience. He brought this up when considering the gray stones surrounding the house as well as the fungi on the walls. This made me weary, as I was now further examining why he was so superstitious about the house more systematically.

The more I thought about the books that we had been pouring over, the more I realized that they all were concerning the character of phantasm. Among these were the Belphegor of Machiavelli, the Ververt of Chartreuse of Gresset, the Heaven and Hell of Swedenborg, the Subterranean Voyage of Nicholas Klimm of Holberg, and some others, all fantastic in character.

And then it came to pass that day in which Mr. Usher informed me of lady Madeline's death. He proposed that we preserve her body for a fortnight in one of several of the vaults contained within the main walls of the house. This precaution was taken mainly because the family's burial ground was a rather remote and exposed one, which would still take some time to get to.

I then helped Usher place the body in its entombment. The vault that we placed the coffin in was small and damp and had an oppressive atmosphere. This vault was placed immediately below the apartment which I had been sleeping in and would never let any light in. At the entrance was a massive iron door because the room used to be used to keep combustible materials.

Once we had placed the coffin in its vault, we finally opened it, and I saw that there was more similitude between her and her brother than I had originally noticed. When I pointed this out, Usher informed me that the two were actually twins. I reexamined her one last time and noticed that there was still some blush to be seen in her face. It was at this point that we closed up the coffin again and went back into the less gloomy apartments of the house.

Some days had now passed since we put the sister to rest. At this point, Usher started to change dramatically. He started to pace wildly throughout the various rooms of the house, and his face became more pallid and lifeless than it had been before. Whatever spark there had been in his eyes was gone now, and he started to act and speak with much more anxiety and terror. His mind was becoming so agitated that I wondered if he had been keeping back some secret from me. He seemed to be going mad. I noticed him gazing at nothing for hours as if he had been listening to some imaginary sound. Eventually, this condition of his started to metastasize throughout my own being, and his superstitions started to become my own.

It wasn't until about the seventh or eighth night since we had placed lady Madeline in her tomb that this feeling of dread truly started to take over my spirit. When it did start to come on, I wanted to blame it on the dreadful furniture within the room. Regardless, a tremor started to come over me that eventually overcame me entirely. As the storm of the night passed on and the terror grew inside of me, I finally decided to throw some clothes on and paced to and fro throughout the apartment.

During the course of my pacing, Usher eventually walked into the room, bearing a lantern. He looked mad when walking in. A reserved hysteria marked his countenance. "And you have not seen it?" he then asked me. He proceeded to throw one of his casements out of the window in the room into the storm at this point.

As he did this, the fury of the storm's wind almost lifted us off of our feet. Looking outside, no stars and no moon were visible, and none of the objects around us was either, but we could see the unnatural light that surrounded the mansion on all sides. Usher then closed the window to keep the cold air out and proposed that we read one of his favorite romances.

It was Sir Lancelot Canning's Mad Trist that Usher picked out for us. I did not agree with his choice, finding this book a bit too lofty and spiritual for my own taste. Nevertheless, this was the only book at hand, so I decided to play along. We finally came to the part of the story in which Ethelred, the hero of Trist, makes his entrance into the hermit's quarters by force. At this point, Ethelred was drunk, and the rain was starting to pour on his shoulders. He feared that the tempest was starting to come on too strong and wanted to get into the hermit's quarters before any more time had passed. There was then an echo mentioned in the story, which mirrored the strange noises that were coming from various parts of the house of Usher throughout this storm. As this fictional echo grew louder, so did the actual noises of the storm outside.

We continued the story regardless, and when Ethelred entered the room of the hermit, he was not met by the hermit himself but instead by a fire breathing dragon that guarded a palace of gold with a silver floor. It was then that Ethelred hit the dragon upon its head and that the dragon fell down defeated, letting out a screech that nearly left Ethelred deaf.

Though I felt a strange admixture of fear and wonder at this passage, I tried my best to not project this mixed feeling outwards with Usher, being already so distraught, near me. Usher turned his chair to point towards the chamber door. His head started to drop toward his chest, and he started to rock back and forth in his chair. I resumed our reading.

And then it came to pass that the dragon's champion saw a bronze shield on the wall of the palace and took it for himself, dissolving the enchantment that it had with it in the process. He then cleared the carcass out, and with this, a terrible ringing sound started to make itself audible throughout the palace.

I rushed over to Usher at his chair, and as I placed my hand upon his shoulder, a shudder metastasized throughout his entire body. He then started to speak in a low murmur, as if he was not conscious of my presence. It was at this point that

I bent over his body, listening closely to every word that he spoke.

"Oh, pity me, what a miserable wretch I am," he started. "I dared not to speak, but we have put her living in the tomb! I heard her first movements in the chamber a few days ago, and I dared not to speak, but when I heard of the breaking of the hermit's door, the death cry of the dragon, and the clashing of the shield, I really heard the rendering of her coffin followed by the grating of her iron hinges and her struggles within the arch of the tomb. Where will I go now? She will kill me when she finds me now."

As if he were superhuman in this last utterance, those panels that he had been facing now started to slowly draw themselves back. Then, from the blackness that followed out come the enshrouded figure of lady Madeline of Usher. All of her white robes were stained with blood, suggesting some sort of struggle over her emaciated frame. She drifted to and fro for a moment in front of her brother, moaning in agonizing cries that only someone in their final hours could produce. Upon seeing this, Usher fell to the ground dead, killed by the very terror he had been anticipating.

It was at this point that I fled the house, with the tempest still roaring outside. Through the clouds, I saw a blood red moon. I then looked back towards the house and saw a violent whirlwind orbing itself and all of its fierce breath around the house, and finally bringing its walls down. And with a long shouting of the winds outside came the ultimate fall of the House of Usher.

Two: The Monkey's Paw

By: W.W Jacobs

It was a cold and wet night outside, but inside of a small parlor in Lakes Nam villa sat a father and his son playing chess by the fireside. The father in this game was choosing moves so dangerous to his king that even the onlookers stopped to criticize his strategies.

Finally, Mr. White's son started to catch on to these mistakes and eventually checked him. At this point, Mr. White started to complain about the commute involved in getting out to the remote place in which they were quartered. Hardly listening, his wife told him that he might win the next game.

"There he is," said Herbert White as loud footsteps were heard coming to the door. There came a tall, burly man by the name of Sergeant Major Morris. Upon arrival, Sergeant Morris shook hands with everyone there. They all proceeded to sit by the fire, with Sergeant Morris providing whiskey and tumblers.

As the night wore on and Sergeant Morris drank more and more, his eyes got wider as he spoke, and the entire party was increasingly transfixed by his strange tales of foreign lands and peoples. They wanted to know more and more about the sergeant's life and experiences in proportion to how much information he shared.

Mr. White pointed out that it had been 21 years that the Sergeant had been in the service and that he had just been an average warehouse worker beforehand. Mrs. White thought that he had incurred little injuries throughout living in India for over two decades, at least as far as she could see. "I would like to go to India myself," the old man said to which the sergeant replied, "you are better where you are."

"I would at least like to see the temples and buildings," the old man continued. "What was that thing that you told me about once, the monkey's paw?" "It's nothing to be concerned about," said the sergeant. "Monkey's paw?" said

Mrs. White. "Well, it's just a little—magic—you might call it," said the sergeant. The three hosts now started to lean into the sergeant, watching for this paw. Out the sergeant pulled the dried paw from his pocket, and Mrs. White drew back in horror, while the youngest White took the paw immediately out of curiosity.

"What is so special about it?" Mrs. Smith asked. "It has had a spell put on it by a fakir," said the sergeant. "He wanted to prove a point that fate controlled all of our lives, so he gave it three fingers and created it for three different men who could each take three wishes from it." "The man who owned this paw before me had his own three wishes. I do not know what the first two were, but the third one was for death, which is the reason that I got this paw in the first place."

The sergeant went on to share that he had already taken his three wishes from the paw. The Whites, still feeling somber from the information of the death, asked why he still had it. He explained that he had some intention of selling it, but no one ever wanted to buy it, either because they did not believe in its authenticity or wanted to only use it without buying it.

Mr. White asked the sergeant, "If you could have another three wishes, would you take them?" The sergeant replied, "I'm just not sure." Then, the sergeant abruptly threw the paw into the fire. Stunned, Mr. White snatched it out as quickly as he could. "You would do well to let it burn, Mr. White," said the sergeant. "No, if you do not want it, then I will take it," replied Mr. White.

"I'm warning you," started the sergeant, "if you do not leave the paw in the fire like a sensible person, then there are going to be severe consequences." "I'm keeping it. Show me how to use it," said Mr. White. "Alright, but I did warn you. Hold the paw up in your right hand and make your wish out loud." "If you must wish, at least wish for something sensible."

Not taking heed of the sergeant's warning, Mr. Smith kept the paw in his pocket. He then invited the sergeant to come and have dinner with his family in the dining room. After they had finished eating, they all went back into the living room, and the three in the family listened to a second instalment of the sergeant's tales from India. It was at this point that Herbert, the youngest in the family, made the point that if the anecdote about the monkey's paw was not more truthful than any of the stories about India then it could be more or less disregarded.

"I only gave him very little for the paw," said Mr. White to his wife, who had a scrutinous look on her face. Then it came to pass that Herbert got very excited, exclaiming loudly "we are going to be rich! Nothing will stand in our way now that we have these wishes to use! Wish to be emperor, Dad, that way none of us can be henpecked."

"No, I did agree with the sergeant's part about being sensible. I still do not know what exactly to wish for, however," said the father. Herbert told his father to wish for two hundred pounds, then went into the other room and pounded out a small few very impressive chords on the piano. "I wish for two hundred pounds," said the old man.

As soon as these words were uttered, a screech escaped Mr. White's mouth, and the piano playing came to a halt at once. "It moved," he cried out. "It twisted in my hand like a snake as soon as I wished on it."

"Well, I still see no money," said Herbert. "I guess there is really no harm done. Though it did kind of shock me all the same," Mr. White replied. The two men then smoked their pipes as a storm roared on outside. Herbert asserted that Mr. White would probably see the money when he woke up first thing in the morning. He also felt that they would all pay dearly for the ill-gotten gains. The room was usually silent and motionless for the remainder of the night.

The next morning, Herbert was the first to get up and see the monkey's paw placed carelessly on the kitchen table, with no apparent esteem held in its virtue. The air in the room was prosaic and motionless. Mrs. White was incensed when she found that no money had come out of the ordeal, exclaiming that all soldiers were the same and that they had wasted all of last evening being duped by a kiniver. "Morris said that things would happen naturally," started Mr. White, "and that we all might contribute to coincidence." It was this time that Herbert headed out the door. His mother watched him until he turned around the end of the street.

Mr. White was convinced that the thing had moved in his hand. He kept going on and on about it to his still unconvinced wife, and she was simply going about her business until she froze in her tracks; she veered out the window into the bright day outside and saw a man looking into the house with great clothes and a glossy hat. She immediately thought of the two hundred pounds when she beheld this sight. He was walking to and fro in front of the gate. It wasn't until the fourth time he had passed it that he finally decided to open it. When she saw this, she took off her apron and headed towards the front door.

She brought him into the main room and, after a hesitation of a few seconds, asked him why he had come. He said that he had been sent by Maw and Meggins. She was stunned upon hearing this news. Mr. White now entered the room and started, "Don't jump to conclusions, I'm sure he is here with good news. Isn't that right?" he turned to the man. "Is he hurt at all?"

"Badly hurt," replied the man. "But he is in no pain." At first, Mrs. White was extremely relieved to hear this but then caught on to the intimation included within the statement. "He got caught up in the machinery," the visitor went on to say in a low, somber tone. "Caught up in the machinery?

What could you possibly mean by that?" asked Mrs. White. "Yes," started Mr. White looking towards his wife, "caught up in the machinery." "We're sorry. This is just so hard for us because he was our only son," he then said to the visitor.

"I would like to offer my condolences," said the visitor. "Please do not kill the messenger. I was sent here by the firm to provide some comfort for you people." He was met with no reply. The wife's face was pallid and still, and the harrowing words of the sergeant tolled on and on within the confines of the husband's skull.

"Maw and Meggins claims no share of the responsibility. It was a simple workplace accident that was in no way brought about by negligence. We do, however, still want to offer you some capital as a consolation for your son's great service to the company. We've decided on the sum of two hundred pounds for this compensation," said the visitor. As soon as these words passed through the lips of the visitor, the old man fell to the ground.

After the burial, the couple returned to the house. A resigned and silent character fell over the property from that day forward. It was the type of reserve and silence that can only be found in the houses of older people who have lost everything, which is often mistaken for apathy. Days and days would go by at times without them saying so much as a word to one another.

It was about a week after the death that Mr. White heard his wife leaving the bed in the dark of the night. He tried to get her back in bed but to no avail. She was desirous of the monkey's paw. "The paw," she started, "where is it?"

"It's in the parlor. Why?"

"Why didn't I think of it before? We can use the other two wishes."

"Wasn't one enough?"

"God no, go down there and wish our boy back to life."

"Get back to bed. You are not thinking about what you are saying."

"What do you mean? We just had one wish granted, why wouldn't we get the second one granted as well? Go down there and get that wish granted." She demanded, pulling him by the arm to the door.

The parlor was completely dark, and he had difficulties finding his way to the table on which the paw was located. His wife told him to hurry up and make the wish. While he still had apprehension towards doing so, he did not want to upset his already insatiate wife. Finally, holding the paw in hand, he proclaimed, "I wish my son to be alive yet again." He then sank into his chair as the woman opened the blinds in the room.

He continued to sit in the same spot until the cold chilled him considerably. They had lit a candle which was now providing oscillations of light for the room in which he saw his wife's profile looking through the window. He then went back to bed, with the wife following him shortly after. They both lay silently in the oppressive darkness of the night from that point on, either one of them hardly sleeping at all.

In the night, Mr. White walked down to the base of the staircase. When he got there, the match that he had lit to light the candle on the lower level went out, and just as this had happened, he heard a knock on the front door. He stood there motionless for a brief period of time. It was not until the third knock that he finally decided to act, preferring to run back upstairs to his room rather than answer it.

"What is that?" the wife asked.

"Just a rat."

The knock continued, pervading throughout the entire house.

"It's Herbert!" she screamed out loud. "That's Herbert!"

She started to run towards the front door, however her husband caught her by the arm.

"What do you think you are doing?" he asked.

"It's our boy, Herbert. We need to let him in."

"No, don't let him in."

"Don't be afraid of your own son. Let me go. I'm coming, Herbert! I'm coming for you!" she said as she was breaking out of her husband's grip.

She raced down the stairs with her husband calling to her from behind. The knocking on the door was only growing in frequency and intensity. Once she got to the door, she could not find the bolt, so she called out to her husband to come and look for it, but he was already on the ground looking with all his energy for the monkey's paw.

The pounding on the door only grew and grew as the man was on the floor in search of the paw. He could suddenly hear a screeching of the chair on the floor as it had been propped up by his wife, and the intruder from outside was still banging at the door. The bolt slowly started to slip back with every passing knock and eventually came all the way undone. It was in this very moment that Mr. White finally found the paw on the ground and breathed his third and final wish into it.

All of the sudden the knocking had completely ceased, though vague echoes of it were still reverberating all throughout the house. The chair then drew back, and the door opened completely, welcoming in a cold wind with it. At that point, he followed his wife out of the door into the light outside, through the gate and past the street they inhabited.

Three: Ligeia

By: Edgar Allen Poe

I honestly cannot remember when it was that I first met Ligeia. This may be due to the fact that my memory is waning with the years, but, then again, it could also be because of the fact that her low musical language made steady and consistent passes on my spirit, in a way that I did not see until much later on. I do believe, at any rate, that I met her originally in an old, despondent city by the Rhine. I never remembered or even learned of her family name. It was that of an almost extinct family. I had never asked of this name either. This would eventually prove to infect our marriage with ill omens from its onset.

On the topic of Ligeia, the person, however, my memory never fails me. She was tall and thin, almost emaciated in her later days, and so very light in her footfall. Her features were not those of the classically beautiful, but, as Bacon famously pointed out, "There is no exquisite beauty without some strangeness in the proportion." Her skin was ivory, contrasted with ebony hair which seemed all the more stunning against her long forehead.

Her eyes glowed vividly. While there are no examples of more beautiful eyes in remote antiquity, hers were a pair with a beauty that was truly stuck out of time. There are simply no means of surpassing the vast latitude of my ignorance of the spiritual enough to do charity to her look in expressing it.

Her brows took on the same intensity of her hair. It is still those eyes, however, that I revered the most, and that still stick with me the most to this day. I always find that feeling of being on the verge of remembering the facts yet not being able to find them to be very disquieting ones. This is always my feeling when trying to recall the full expression of Ligeia's eyes, never quite being able to achieve what I sought out to. Right after she had passed, I started to see her eyes in all of the orbs that I came across. In all of these orbs, I saw both her scrutiny and her will.

There was one thing that was very odd, and very paradoxical, about Ligeia's character: she was at once the calmest woman that I had ever met and the most severely debilitated by turbulence and anxiety. Her calm was outward, while her consternation metastasized throughout the whole of her inner life. While it was seldom that she was ever gripped by passions, the ones that would arise would always be incredibly strong and stern ones, gripping her will with iron and transforming her into a tyrant. Of those passions, I could never form any real estimate, except by the expression in her eyes, as well as those of the voice and of her actions.

The learning of Ligeia was immense and expansive. In the classical tongues of Europe, she was fluent and never had difficulties in the study regardless of the language used or the topics at hand. It was not until later in our marriage, however, once I had noticed her proficiency in all fields, that I started to more properly recognize her erudition at length. Once I started to see the value in her education, I finally let my guard down and allowed her to guide me through any further metaphysical speculation in the future.

After some time spent with her guiding my intellectual life, she grew ill, and her eyes started to pour over the books she had with less and less vivacity as time went on. Those same eyes started to shine less vividly, and her skin turned much colder and more pallid. It was at this point that I started to see that the shadow of death was closing in upon her, though she fought this shadow with greater audacity than I had ever seen her fight with before. It came to pass that her struggle for existence became more vivid for me than did my own. Her voice grew thinner and softer as I awaited her departure with horrible anticipation.

While I never doubted that she did love me, it was not until she died that I could finally appreciate the depth and the breadth of this love. It was only then that I came to recall just how often she had extolled to me her admiration and appreciation toward me. I will not speak any more on this love which I did not deserve, nor can I properly express her will to live that was now diminishing.

And now on her deathbed, mention was made of the conqueror worm. She asked whether or not the worm was ever conquered itself. She knew that no living man was aware of the worm's vigor, so she started to question just what it could do.

She was losing more and more energy, unable at last even to support her own arms. Her own voice grew weaker and weaker as she spoke of the weak wills of those who had already succumbed to death. She finally died, and I was determined that I could no longer dwell in my desolate and isolated quarters off of the Rhine. Ligeia left me no shortage of wealth, so I was eventually able to get a new house in a very secluded part of England. The gloom and isolation of the building were in line with my melancholic spirits at that time, though I eventually gave the property a regal pomp in its decoration from within. All of the frivolous that I poured into the dwelling took my mind off of all the grief temporarily. There was one chamber in particular that I should mention here, from which I led my bride and successor of Ligeia Lady Rowena Trevanion to the altar.

I can still remember each and every detail of that bridal chamber. On the whole, it was much loftier and Venetian than any of the other parts of the house. Specimens of semi-Gothic and semi-Druidical devices were everywhere throughout the apartment.

There were also a few ottomans along with a golden candelabra. It also had a bridal couch of another eastern model. Tapestry was curtained over the bed, and there were ghastly forms, presumably Norman, peppered throughout the entire room.

It was within this bridal chamber that I passed the first few months of my marriage to Lady Rowena. While there was little tension between the two of us, there still remained her dislike of her temper coupled with her subsequent shunning of me between us. My hatred toward her only grew more and more demonic as I recalled more and more of Ligeia's more agreeable nature. My spirit started slowly to burn with flames greater than her own.

During the second month of our marriage, Lady Rowena was struck with a sudden illness, which left her droning half sensibly in a half-wakeful state of mind for a considerable amount of time, but not long after she was struck with a second illness, this one being more severe and doing damage to her frame which would prove to be irreversible. This illness, like the previous one, baffled all of her physicians, and her temper became even more irritable than it had been before. While she was still able to speak, though only lightly, after having had become a sufferer of this illness, she preferred to stick to motions to communicate beyond this point.

It was one night in September that she started to press me on the matter of her illness harder than before. She was feeling increasingly anxious and faint and needed more assistance then she usually had. After speaking with her, I poured her a glass of wine and pressed it to her lips. She then felt partially healed, so I took some of the wine for myself.

It was right after she had drunk this wine, however, that her condition started to deteriorate dramatically. That night some help and I prepared her tomb, and the next night after I sat with her draped body in the same room that I had married her in. As I looked on at her lifeless cadaver, I could only think of Ligeia. That night, I slept watching the body. A sound eventually came about that would only be explained later on. I then saw some color still left in her face and realized that Rowena was still living. I tried with no aid to keep her alive but to no avail. The coldness of death once again overcame her body, and I was again made content with passing visions of Ligeia.

An hour passed by, and I heard the same noise again. I went over to the body and saw a tremor in its lips coupled with more color in its face. I was astonished, but then the coldness came back yet another time, just as quickly as it had before.

Again, I subsided back into thinking of Ligeia. And again, it came to pass this repeated process of revivification several times throughout the night. Hers was a flame which would not simply be extinguished, and I was forced to experience the emotional vicissitudes of the night. As this continued to happen, I stopped getting up. I simply remained on the ottoman until in one of these cycles, she showed more life in her than she had in any of the others.

I eventually looked up only to be surprised by a shadowy figure in the center of the room. I stared transfixed into it, wondering whether or not it could have been Rowena. The more I looked on, the taller the figure seemed to become, and all the darker its hair. I wondered if Rowena had taken up these characteristics until all of the sudden the figure had come face to face with me. Nonplussed, I finally realized that the figure had been Ligeia all along.

Four: The Lake

By: Ray Bradbury

The waves of the lake were closing me off from the rest of the world. They provided a green silence that separates me from the speech of my Mom and of the other children. When I would leave the lake, the rest of the world would be waiting for me.

I was running on the beach when Mama stopped me and told me to dry myself off with a towel. I then stood there putting on my sweater while the beads of waters on my arms were quickly becoming goosebumps.

I then watched the waves of the lake with my sweater on. They were collapsing in on themselves with elegance and consistency. It was September at that time and the whole world was becoming much more dismal around me. There was less movement in the trees, and the other children stopped playing outside.

The food stands that neighbored the beach in the summer months were all being boarded up now. Even some of the stationery businesses were now boarding themselves up. The musical wind blew the sand violently around the town on the beach.

I stood there on the beach with Mama. All of the other kids were at school at the time, but I was preparing to take a train across the country. I remember telling Mama that I wanted to stay on the beach forever. I asked her if I could go to the water one last time. She told me that I could, but I could still not get in. The closer I came to the shore, the smaller she looked behind me, and the more alone I felt.

Once I saw that I was alone out there, I got into the water. I submerged myself up to my stomach in the chilly water. It is always strange how water can make your body feel almost sawed between where you are submerged in it and where you are not.

It was at this point that I remembered Tally, a twelve-year-old girl I had swum with over the summer. I also remembered how the lifeguard came to try to save her, how her mother screamed, and how she never got out of the water alive. That very same girl who had helped me in school and who had played ball with me at home had also been claimed by the lake. The autumnal gloom continued to pervade over the scene.

I started to call her name because I suppose that I still could not believe that she was really gone. I had, after all, loved her very much. This was not an ordinary love though. It was one that transcended any normal bodily and moral proclivities, and I was reminded of it by the sight of the same lake that had taken her under.

I called out her name one last time before leaving. It was at this point that I noticed that the cold water had gotten onto my face. I then returned to the shore, building a sand castle for my departed friend for about half an hour before finally leaving. I only built half of this though, leaving the other half to be completed by Tally. Walking away, I looked back to see the waves smooth out the castle once and for all.

I then moved on a train. It is so funny how forgetful trains really are, putting all things behind themselves as they go by. We moved to Sacramento, where I spent the rest of my youth, going through school to college, where I met who was to eventually become my wife.

Margaret, my wife, suggested that we go back to that lake, Lake Bluff, for our honeymoon. We went, and she kept me calm throughout the process of having all of my memories come back anew.

All of the faces I had once known had either changed beyond recognition or had been replaced with new ones. When Margaret and I finally walked around the town, there was no one around who I could at all recognize.

On one of the last days of our stay, we went to the same beach. It was around that same time of the year, so very few people were there. The fierce wind met us immediately upon our arrival as if it had been in waiting. It was late in the day, and most of the children had already gone home. Only men and women remained, and I almost saw Mama in a few of the women.

Looking toward the shore, I saw a lifeguard. He was steering a boat toward the shore and was carrying something in his arms. I stood there stunned for a few moments, the wind suddenly ceasing its persistent attack. I told Margaret to stay where she was.

I went over to where the lifeguard was standing, and as I walked, he looked me in the eyes. He had a look of disbelief and of disgust in his eyes. I asked him what it was that he had. "It's strange to see," he replied. "She has been dead for a very long time."

"I would estimate that she has been down here for 10 years. There have been 12 other children who have drowned here within that time span, but all of their bodies have been recovered. This one—this one has evaded us for a very long time."

I looked at the gray bag that the body was presumably in and told him to open it. I am still not quite sure why I did this, but, regardless, he initially did not want to grant me this macabre request. I think it must have been the terrified expression on my face that he saw at that moment that must have convinced him to unveil the corpse, which he only did slightly. The one small glance that I got of the remains was enough.

The beach was deserted at this point. The cold autumn winds were back, and the lifeguard informed me that she had been found in a shallow section of the beach. People grow. I had grown, but the fact that she was going to be locked into that being of an adolescent girl for all time gave me a strange admixture of comfort and grief when thinking of her life. The guard tied up the sack again.

I stood there on the beach alone. This really was the same spot where she had died, and now, but some strange twist of fortune, I had been brought back here with serendipity in order to watch her lifeless cadaver be pulled from its resting spot.

I looked back at the water. To my surprise, I saw half of a sand castle, much like the ones Tabby and I used to build. I walked closer to it and noticed some small footprints heading into the water and never returning, a one-way passage into the icy waters which were to claim my friend's life. I promised her that I would finish the other half of the castle, which I sat down and did. Once it was finished, I got up and walked back to Margaret. Once I got to her, I looked back to see that this castle, unlike the last, was still there, complete on the beach.

Five: The Legend of Sleepy Hollow

By: Washington Irving

In one of the many coves that indent the eastern shore of the Hudson, there lies a port town by the name of Tarrytown. This name was given by the housewives of an adjacent village who always complained of their husbands spending all of their time at the tavern of the town. About two miles outside of this town, there lies a valley which may be one of the quieter places on the globe. The only sounds that invade this space are the slow murmurings of a brook and the occasional tappings of a woodpecker. This silence made this valley the perfect refuge from the needless stressors and cares of this world.

The town's residents called the place Sleepy Hollow, and the young men of the town were known as the Sleepy Hollow Boys. The atmosphere surrounding the place was drowsy and dreamy, and the whole of the place was suspected to be under the power of some sort of witchery. This power had a spell over the town's people, making them prone to visions and trances. Superstition and folklore surrounded the place, making it a favorite scene of gambols.

The commander in chief of all of these forces of the air is, however, the headless ghost of a Hessian trooper. Rumor has it that this trooper's head was taken off by a cannonball during the revolutionary war. He haunts the valley, and townsfolk assert that he revisits the same battleground each and every night after dark in search of the head. To locals, this ghost goes by the name of the Headless Horseman of Sleepy Hollow.

It does not take long for anyone to be imbibed with the dreamy propensity of the valley. This propensity is by no means limited just to the natives of the region. Any visitors take very little time to inhale the witching influence of the air and to grow much more imaginative. This is some dark, spiritual force that seeps into the souls of all of the people who find themselves living here. Even those who move to this place with no proclivity towards neuroticism or superstition are soon imbibed with this spirit not long after settling down. Here the question of relative hysteria presents itself: If everyone around a body is crazed, then how will that body know sane from insane?

Here, the customs and mannerisms of the people remained more or less fixed in time. This differs widely from the happenings of the larger cities in New York state that are always renewed by the thought and spirit of foreign immigrants. Here, year after year, you will see the same trees and the same landscapes, as well as the same practices and dogmas of the people. The colloquial veins of these people run slower in their blood flow, making the facts that do present themselves stick around all the more.

There was a man in the town of Sleepy Hollow who went by the name of Ichabod Crane. His business in the town was to educate the children. He was a tall man from Connecticut and had long arms and a small head. From the side, this man took on much the same profile of a scarecrow. The schoolhouse that Ichabod taught in was a modest one made out of old and tattered logs. This was a rather lonely place for him, but his students kept him all the company that he needed during the day, though he would tend to be very hard on them at times.

Ichabod was not a harsh or severe disciplinarian though. He was fair in his judgments with the children, always helping the weak when they were up against the strong. He carried out all of his judgments with careful deliberation and only came to the wisest and most just conclusions that he could muster, after and only after weighing and examining all of the evidence at hand, remaining impartial throughout the process and taking all of the issues at hand on case by case basis. His pupils took notice of this trait and emulated their master. In maintaining this trait of good judgment, which is very often much too hard for most to keep, Ichabod had created a generation of great deliberators who would go on to develop their abilities in determining fairness in their futures.

After school hours, Ichabod would even spend time with some of the larger boys, and often walk the smaller ones home, usually being invited in for food by the women of these houses. He would even go so far as to board with some of these families for weeks at a time. While this habit may have been strange in a family man tied down by the weights of his children and spouse, it was never met with resistance. Ichabod's staying with other families became a welcomed happening for many families within the community.

Many of his patrons found the cost of schooling to be a large burden, and also found schoolmasters to be boring. For this reason, Ichabod always tried to make himself as useful as he could to these people to ensure their continued business. It was always the mothers that he would have to worry about the most, but he was especially able to win over the favor of the females that patronized him.

He was also the choirmaster of his neighborhood. This additional occupation brought him in even more income, though not very much more. This position came naturally to him because he was endowed with a singing voice that would carry over all others in the town. On Sundays, he would direct the church choir, his voice emanating over and above all others in the town. It was by this occupation that he would eventually prove to make most of his connections with the townspeople. Those who he met at the schoolyard were either children or wanted nothing further to do with him, but all were welcoming at church, and it was here that he felt most at home among the other members of his community.

Among the women of the neighborhood, the schoolmaster was always a personage of great importance. Ichabod, only being surpassed in learning by the person himself, won over the favor of the ladies that he came into contact with. When contrasted with the rougher country brutes of the rural area, he seemed quite gifted and quite useful. It would be this differentiation that would give him both his biggest rewards and his biggest headaches in the long run. He became at once very admired and still very unwelcomed, almost feared by some because of his learning.

There was much talk centered around him within the town. The women found his erudition charming. He had read many books through and was especially familiar with the works of Cotton Mather. He was a very esteemed individual among the townsfolk, but the strange witchery of the entire town did still follow him around just as it did all of the others.

He enjoyed listening to the folklore just as much as all of the other townsfolk. They would all spend many nights sharing tales of goblins, witchcraft, the Headless Horseman, and the like. Ichabod would be so affected by these tales that he often feared that he was going to be attacked when he saw it coming least by one of these characters. Ichabod, being naturally drawn to fiction and the like from a rather early age, found these tales extremely intriguing and was immediately dominated in his thoughts by them.

Whatever these fears Ichabod would have at night were, they would all come to subside each and every morning. There was one of the of the musical disciples of the town that Ichabod eventually noticed among others though. This was Katrina Van Tassel, the only daughter of a well off Dutch farmer in the area. Katrina was an eighteen-year-old and a bit of a coquette. Ichabod found this girl's fickleness attractive in a way that he could not exactly pinpoint and was immediately set in his mind on winning her over as soon as he had met her.

This girl caught Ichabod's attention and would not let go. Her father, Old Baltus Van Tassel, was a liberal farmer with a contented heart and a thriving spirit. They lived in abundance on a farm off of the banks of the Hudson River. This property of theirs was teaming with animal life, from pigeons and foxes scattered throughout the front of the property to geese and frogs inhabiting the adjoining pond.

Ichabod thought about eating all of these animals as he passed by each and every one. He also fantasized about setting up a life in this place for himself with Katrina. She was the rightful heir to the property, and he wanted to share all of the abundances he saw around him with her. He imagined the two of them with a large family of children. When he, at last, entered the house itself, his heart immediately became set on it.

From the moment that Ichabod laid eyes on the interior of the house, he made up his mind to win over the affection of Katrina with everything in his power. He was reminded of the old knight's tales, in which the heroes were assigned to fight off dragons, giants, enchanters, and the like to get whatever it was that they were after. Ichabod's task was simple in comparison: to win over the heart of a country coquette. Simplicity does not, in this case as in many others, imply ease, however. In order to accomplish his goal, he would first need to pass through quite an impressive labyrinth of whims and caprices. Ichabod was no hero, after all. He was, and always had been, fine by himself and did very little out of his own way to impress others, whether they were men or women. He felt unnatural actively scheming on ways in which to impress this girl, and wondered actively why it was exactly that he was so transfixed on winning her over. He had never come across another person who changed in demeanor so frequently, a quality that proved to at once both frustrate him beyond what he initially anticipated and also kept him guessing more and for longer than he would have otherwise.

Ichabod was not without competition though. His most prominent competitor was a young man by the name of Brom Van Brunt. Van Brunt was a country boy, well built with short, curly hair. The townsfolk referred to him as Brom Bones and his gang, and he got a great reputation as being a very fair group. Brom was physically very strong and handled himself much in the same manner as that of a brute, which intimidated some while others were easily able to look through it as the true weakness that it was, resultant of having no real control over his own faculties, and therefore enslaving himself by his own emotions, the baser and more primitive they were, the more they imprisoned him.

Van Brunt had courted Katrina in the past, and she was not entirely averse to these advances, occasionally entertaining him with a certain amount of excitement. This was the rival that Ichabod had to contend with and a very formidable one at that.

To decide to take on Van Brunt face to face would be madness. For this reason, Ichabod made all of his advancements toward Katrina in a quiet, insinuating manner. He would do so by excusing his visits to the house by his character of the schoolmaster. Balt Van Tassel was an easy man to please, and would generally let his daughter get away with anything she wanted to do. This is why Ichabod had so much success with this tactic. The old man would simply never prohibit his visits. His daughter somewhat shared this agreeable nature. It did not take Ichabod very long at all to notice that one of her bigger faults lay in the fact that she could never say "no" to anyone that would bother her. It is a trait that is common in the fairer sex but always proves to be detrimental to the health of marriages.

Each and every woman has her own unique heart, with its own peculiar sensibilities. There are means of taking ownership of a heart with only one port of entry that differs from means of taking ownership of one with several. As far as keeping the favor of these hearts is concerned, however, it is keeping that of the one with several that deserves more praise. To win a thousand common hearts deserves some public admiration, but to win over just one of a coquette makes one a heroic figure. Brom was never able to complete this task, as soon as Ichabod entered Katrina's life, her favor was immediately directed at him. This naturally made Brom agitated, and his threats directed at Ichabod only multiplied with the passage of time. The plain fact of the matter is that Katrina was more attracted to Ichabod than she was to Brom. There is a possibility that this was due to the stability of Ichabod's character, which would act as something of an anchor for her own emotions as she experienced life and all of its vicissitudes. Brom was never as useful to her because he could control himself no better than she could herself. Possibly even worse, in fact. There is a fair bit of contrast involved in compatibility between people. Two or more parties need to contrast one another in certain areas, in which these parties need assistance and could use some sort of example. Ichabod offered great qualities that were more useful to Katrina than those of Brom were.

These two men went on about their business for some time in this manner without any incident until one autumn day. Ichabod was teaching his class, and all of his students were engaged in study. Then it came to pass that a black man entered the room suddenly. He was on a mule, and the cap on his head resembled that of Mercury. There was a hush that metastasized throughout the classroom as he spoke, inviting Ichabod to a party that night at the Van Tassel residence. He was then on his way, and the classroom erupted yet again in conversation.

The school was let out half an hour early that day, with the children leaving all of their books and other supplies in shambolic condition. Ichabod took this time to clean himself up as well as he could, putting on only the best clothes he could find and taking extra time with toiletries. He wanted to present himself to his mistress as a true cavalier though, so he borrowed a horse for the occasion from an old Dutch farmer named Hans Van Ripper.

It was a clear autumn day, and Ichabod left for the residence on the back of a horse that suited him very well. All of the birds of the area were singing their songs with their usual vivacity, their various colors and hues complimenting the waning colors of the leaves on the trees they inhabited.

As Ichabod moved along his way, he also noticed all of the foods surrounding him, from the apples on the trees to the corn on the stalks and the pumpkins on the vines all around him. As he journeyed along the Hudson that day, he was accompanied by a few amber clouds and a gradual hue from aqua green on the horizon to a deep blue in the middle of the sky. The scene was perfect for everything that it was.

Around evening time, Ichabod finally came across the castle of Heer Van Tassel. He was met there by old farmers, all in excellent attire and with their daughters as company. There were also many young men and boys there, but it was Brom Bones, after all, who was the true hero of the scene. He had arrived on his notoriously ill-tempered horse, Daredevil, that was as ill-tempered and full of mischief as its owner.

The charms that both Brom and Ichabod were met with at the castle were manyfold. Not only were the ladies of the place numerous and very pretty, but they were also welcomed to cakes of various kinds. There were doughnuts and all sorts of pies, as well as broiled shad and baked ham, among many other treats. Ichabod was a grateful and jolly creature, whose face had no other option but then to light up at all of these appetizing sights and smells.

Old Baltus Van Tassel moved among his guests with a countenance of friendliness and jollity at this party. This was usually the case as befits his amiable character. His encounters with his guests were brief but very expressive and agreeable, greeting mostly everyone with a quick shake of the hand and a slap on the shoulder. This was usually the case of his temperament. He carried himself with that effortless dignity that was characteristic only of a man who already had everything that he needed. He had been gifted with a daughter and an estate that would have pleased any man, so he rarely had need of showing bitterness.

The sound of music was now emanating from the common room. The musician was an old, gray-haired man with an instrument as old and as withered as himself. He bowed almost to the ground and lowered his head whenever greeted by the people. Ichabod prided himself on his dancing almost as much as he did on his singing. Not a single fiber in his body remained idle at the party and he always carried himself with the utmost grace. Needless to say, this quality in him attracted the attention of many of the party's guests, Katrina included. Meanwhile, Brom Bones sat in the corner, jealous and sulking. Ichabod was naturally attracted to the sager characters at the party though and subsequently spent much time discussing details of the war with the older people at the party.

This neighborhood that Ichabod found himself in was a rather famous one. Anecdotes of battles and great men abounded throughout this area, as a British and American line of combat ran through the place in the past. Most of these tales were largely false though, as the local storytellers had been given just enough time at this point to make themselves the heroes of all of the stories.

One of these stories centered around a character by the name of Touffue Martling, a Dutchman who had almost taken a British frigate with an old iron gun. There were several others who have been determined by popular opinion to have played decisive roles in the war, most of which were discussed at this party.

All of these tales about soldiers, however, were nothing compared to those about ghosts and apparitions that succeeded. This neighborhood was even more abundant in tales of these kinds. This neighborhood was such a good home to these tales because it allowed them time to grow and to stick in the minds of the inhabitants. In most villages, for example, tales of this nature are usually overrun by different tales and or just plain gossip before they can even get a foothold on the vernacular.

It was the very vicinity of Sleepy Hollow that led to all of these stories of the supernatural though. There was a contagion in the air of the supernatural, that had a profound effect on the town and its inhabitants. Among the storied ghosts of the town there including that of Major Andre, and that of the woman in white, that was said to haunt the river rock by nightfall. The most famous of these ghosts was undoubtedly that of the headless horseman though. This spirit was said to patrol the countryside at night, tethering his horses on the gravestones of the graveyard.

The church circumjacent to the town was made a favorite haunt for troubled spirits by its location alone. It stood on its own steep hill, with whitewashed walls announcing themselves boldly to the local area, its green lawn beside the bank of the Hudson. One tale was told of old Brouwer in this setting, who met the headless horseman despite his not believing in spirits of any kinds. The horseman, after turning into a skeleton, threw old Brouwer into the brook below and sprang over the rooftops with a clap of thunder.

This story was topped by one of Brom Bones, who shared that he had been overtaken by the horseman on his way back to the town one night. He offered to race him, with the prize being a bowl of punch for the victor. Brom claimed that he was about to win until the Hessian bolted off in the other direction last minute, leaving a flash of fire in his wake. All of these tales sank deep into Ichabod's mind. He repaid his fellow party goers with some of the tales of Cotton Mather.

The people started to leave the party with haste. The old farmers started to get their families into their carriages, and Ichabod followed slowly behind the main vein of the people leaving. Despondent, he wondered if Katrina's interest in him had been a sham after all, and whether or not he actually had a chance to impress her.

It was entering the witching hour of the night. The cold air hit Ichabod with a tenacity that was unrivaled elsewhere in the atmosphere. Across the banks of the Hudson, he could hear the barking of dogs, coupled with the crowing of some birds in the night.

All the stories of ghosts he had heard earlier in the evening started to flood his thoughts. The night started to grow much darker, with the stars above seeming to sink deeper and deeper into the sky. Despondent and lonelier than ever, he crossed by a gigantic tulip tree, fantastic in its limbs. It was this tree that had been connected with Major Andre. This was due to some of the strange sights surrounding it. He passed by this tree, whistling nervously, with no danger, but greater perils lay in front of him.

Around a hundred yards from the tree, a small brook crossed the road and ran into a swamp. There was a cavernous gloom over the area which anyone passing by could never help but to notice. Ichabod's heart started to palpitate upon seeing this stream, and he tried at once to lead his horse across it, but the horse only made a sideways move into the fence bordering the road upon his command. He struggled hard for control of the horse, but the animal was being compelled by some force that was much stronger than Ichabod. Eventually, Ichabod's head was hit by something he could not see. The hairs on the top of his head stood up panicked.

Attacked by some unknown monster he could not see, Ichabod called out, "Who are you?" to which he received no reply. Finally, he started to discern some dimensions of this monster. It appeared to be some kind of horseman, large and mounted on top of a powerful black horse. He tried to ride along on his own horse without causing any trouble. This encounter made Ichabod recall Brom's run-in with the horseman, so he at once doubled his speed in order to escape the situation, but the horseman did the same. Upon seeing this, Ichabod slowed his pace to a walk, only to be again copied by the movement of the horseman. Upon further investigation, Ichabod now realized that this shadowy figure was, in fact, headless, a discovery which even furthered his own sense of terror.

The two were now on the main road that led in and out of Sleepy Hollow. It was at this point that Ichabod's horse started to make more turns into directions opposite of what

Ichabod pressed the animal towards. Here, the horse turned onto a road which led to Sandy Hollow, a neighboring town.

The girths of the saddle started to give way as Ichabod was riding speedily through the Hollow. He eventually resorted to simply holding the beast by the neck, with the saddle falling to the ground below him. He had lost all control of the animal at this point, which seemed to be possessed by some sort of spirit itself increasingly. Almost pathetically, Ichabod continued to ride in this fashion, constantly being jerked back and forth at the creature's whim, for some more time.

An opening in the trees indicated to Ichabod that he was, at last, nearing the church bridge. There was also the reflection of a star in the water below that affirm this suspicion. Upon seeing this sight, Ichabod thought to himself "If I can reach that bridge, I will be safe", recalling the anecdote told by Brom Bones of the horseman giving up the race when arriving at that very same bridge. Just when Ichabod was about to cross this bridge, he could hear the galloping and the effort of the horse coming up closer and closer behind him, even getting the impression of the horse's breath upon the back of his frame. He looked back to see if the horseman was going to retreat at the bridge, much like he did with Brom Bones, but it was then that Ichabod was hit in the head by the head of the horseman, despite his trying to dodge this projectile. His own horse, that of the horseman, and the horseman himself passed Ichabod by as he lay on the ground.

The next morning Ichabod's horse was found without its saddle, cropping the grass outside its master's gate soberly. Ichabod never made an appearance at the schoolyard that day. Breakfast, lunch, and dinner all came about, but on none of these occasions was Ichabod to be found anywhere. All of the schoolboys worried about their schoolmaster's safety, while Hans Van Ripper was concerned about getting his saddle back in his own possession. After some deliberation, they all started off looking for Ichabod on foot. First, they found some traces of him. The saddle was found trampled in the dirt, and some tracks from the horse's hoofs were found on the road, leading up to and beyond the bridge. Below in the water of the brook was found Ichabod's hat, with the smashed pumpkin right next to it.

They then searched the brook thoroughly. They could not, however, find the body of the schoolmaster here. Hans Van

Ripper examined all of Ichabod's worldly possessions in the meantime. These mostly consisted of clothes and a few of his personal books. All of the books and supplies for use within the schoolhouse now belonged to the community. Ichabod had received his quarter's pay a few days before this incident, which had been on his person during, making this sum effectually missing.

The event and the mysterious circumstances surrounding it were, needless to say, the object of much speculation within the church and town throughout the following days. Many of the people congregated around the church and the bridge to speak more among themselves about the event. The stories of Brouwer, Bones, and many others were discussed, making Ichabod's seem like just another in a long stream of folkloristic anecdotes surrounding this mysterious figure. Everyone agreed that it must have been the Hessian that got him and, seeing that Ichabod was just a bachelor, no one continued to think very much of him. The schoolyard was moved to a different area of the town and was then taught by a different pedagogue.

Several years later, an old farmer came to the town with the news that Ichabod Crane was still, in fact, alive, and that he had fled the town out of fear of the Goblin and Hans Van Ripper, as well as out of the disappointment that he was imbued with after having being dismissed by Katrina. He had even studied law within the passing years and had been appointed to the bar. During this time, he had still kept school, as well as served as politician and writer, and had now even been appointed a justice of the Ten Pound Court. Brom Bones, who had always laughed at the story whence it arrived at the part about the pumpkin, was worried upon hearing this news, as he had taken Katrina to the altar in the passing years and did not want his feet stepped on at any point in the future by his former rival. His resentment towards Ichabod lived on with such tenacity that some even suspected him of having some part in the incident.

It was the old country wives who got the final judgement on this matter though, as they usually did on matters such as these. They all unanimously concluded that Ichabod had been taken by some supernatural forces and that no living member of the community should have therefore been looked upon as being suspect in the incident. This story, needless to say, became another favorite of the townspeople and was told over and over again at any and all get together within the town and the adjacent countryside for the years to come. The bridge, in particular, became the subject of much awe among the townsfolk for years to come and was eventually adopted in appearance to curtail people's fear of the landmark. The schoolyard became yet another object of local horror, being deserted and falling into decay, it was suspected of being haunted by the restless spirit of its former master. The ploughboy who then worked nearest to the school continued to sing the melancholy psalms that his former teacher had taught him around the sight for many years to come.

Conclusion

And with that, we have now gone over some of the most important works that history has to offer in the genre of horror fiction. Thank you for making it through to the end of *Short Horror Stories: Supernatural Stories That Are Scarier Than the Dead.*

We have just read through the works of some of the most important horror writers in the history of fiction: W.W. Jacobs, Ray Bradbury, Washington Irving, and Edgar Allan Poe. Horror is one of the most, if not the most, useful genres within fiction as a whole. This is because of the fact that fear is the most powerful emotion that we face as humans. Of all of the things that we get afraid of, there is one thing that affects us most profoundly across all of these areas: the fear of the unknown. In reading horror fiction, we are putting ourselves up against all of the things that we are unaware of, which may put us in a state of unease in the short term, but also makes us analyze what is going on around us more closely and leads to long-term enlightenment.

Also, the fact that these are scary stories does not imply that they have nothing to teach you. While the works of Edgar Allan Poe may never offer any greater moral or educational significance, those of these other authors are usually full to the brim with great information and advice.

Let's hope you enjoyed reading all of these stories. Thank you again for downloading *Short Horror Stories: Supernatural Stories That Are Scarier Than the Dead*.

Connect with us on our Facebook page www.facebook.com/bluesourceandfriends and stay tuned to our latest book promotions and free giveaways.

Printed in Great Britain
by Amazon